KU-176-482

DENNIS DIPP ON GILBERT'S POND

Can Dennis Dipp conquer his fear of water and save Hardley-Skint Hall from the clutches of dastardly Phil Buckett? Dive in and find out!

Nick Warburton was a primary school teacher for ten years before becoming a full-time writer. He has written plays for stage, television and radio, including *Conversations from the Engine Room*, which won the 1985 Radio Times Drama Award. For children, he has written, among others, *The Battle of Baked Bean Alley*, *Normal Nesbitt*, *To Trust a Soldier*, *Ackford's Monster*, *You've Been Noodled!* and *Gladiators Never Blink*. A visiting fellow of University College, Chichester, he is married with a son and lives in Cambridge.

Books by the same author

The Battle of Baked Bean Alley
Flora's Fantastic Revenge

For older readers

Lost in Africa
Ackford's Monster
Normal Nesbitt
To Trust a Soldier
You've Been Noodled!

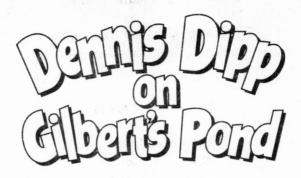

Dennis Dipp on Gilbert's Pond

NICK WARBURTON

Illustrations by

ARTHUR ROBINS

WALKER BOOKS

AND SUBSIDIARIES

LONDON • BOSTON • SYDNEY

For
Rose Carmel

First published 1996 by Walker Books Ltd
87 Vauxhall Walk, London SE11 5HJ

This edition published 2000

2 4 6 8 10 9 7 5 3 1

Text © 1996 Nick Warburton
Illustrations © 1996 Arthur Robins

The right of Nick Warburton to be identified as author of this
work has been asserted by him in accordance with the
Copyright, Designs and Patents Act 1988.

This book has been typeset in Plantin.

Printed and bound in Great Britain by
The Guernsey Press Co. Ltd

British Library Cataloguing in Publication Data
A catalogue record for this book
is available from the British Library.

ISBN 0-7445-7814-0

Contents

Puddles

....

It all began with a bread-and-butter pudding.

Dennis Dipp's dad was a cook in the army. His commander, Colonel Hardley-Skint, thought he made the best bread-and-butter pudding in the entire world. After a specially fine one, he wiped his whiskers and said to Dennis's dad, "Sergeant Dipp, this bread-and-butter pudding is sublime. One day you shall have your reward."

And one day, Sergeant Dipp did. It was an invitation to spend two weeks at the Colonel's home. But the army decided it was time for Dennis's dad to see the dentist, so he couldn't go to Hardley-Skint Hall.

"Then send young Dennis," said the Colonel.

So Sergeant Dipp did. It made him a proud man to think his son would be staying with the Colonel. He told Dennis to write him a postcard telling him all about it. After two days, Dennis took up his pen and thought hard. This is what he wrote:

Having lots of FUN.

Hardley-Skint Hall very POSH.

Posh rooms, posh gardens, posh pictures.

Love, Dennis

One morning Dennis went jogging through the grounds of Hardley-Skint Hall and out into the village. He was careful not to jog in a straight line. Sometimes he swerved and sometimes he did a little leap in the air. He did this to avoid the puddles. Dennis hated treading in puddles.

When he got back to the gates of the Hall, he stopped for a rest. He put his hands on his knees and breathed hard. Between the sounds of his breathing – *whoosh-ah*, *whoosh-ah* – there came a second sound –

scritch-thud, scritch-thud. And this sound was coming from the direction of the Hall.

"Now, what is that?" he said to himself.

He leaned against a large sign on the Hall gates and tried to work it out.

The sign said:

KEEP OUT   GO AWAY
(ESPECIALLY ART DEALERS)
WE DON'T WANT TO KNOW

It had been Mrs Hardley-Skint's idea. There were valuable pictures at Hardley-Skint Hall and the Hardley-Skints didn't want to lose them. To begin with, the sign had said:

KEEP OUT   GO AWAY
(ESPECIALLY CON MEN)

Colonel Hardley-Skint was particularly nervous about con men. However, Mrs Hardley-Skint said that putting "con men" on the sign might be just the thing to attract their attention, so the Colonel had the sign changed to throw them off the scent.

Suddenly, the strange *scritch-thud* sound stopped. Dennis held himself very still, his ears pricked, waiting.

That was when the sign on the gate pushed him over. It didn't do it by itself – the sign pushed him because the gate was swinging open. And the gate was swinging open because somebody had moved it. Dennis fell down flat. Then he rolled on his back and looked up.

A man with shiny black hair was slipping silently through. He was gazing back over his shoulder, so he didn't notice Dennis. He wouldn't have seen him at all if Dennis hadn't squeaked.

"Ow!"

"What are you doing down there?" snapped the man, jumping back with shock.

"Being trodden on," said Dennis.

"You want to be careful," said the man in a

hurt voice. "I might've tripped right over."

Dennis noticed that his hair was as flat and shiny as plastic. He had a small mouth, thin and twisted down, the shape of a nail-clipping.

As Dennis struggled to his feet, the sound started up again – *scritch-thud, scritch-thud*. He looked sharply towards Hardley-Skint Hall.

"What's that?"

"It's a gate," said the man. "Surely you know what a gate is."

"Not the gate. That sound. What is it?"

"Don't know. Nothing to do with me."

"I ought to take a peep," Dennis told him. "The Colonel might need some help."

"Suit yourself," said the man as if he didn't care.

Dennis stepped through the gate. A little way up the drive he came to a large puddle. He stopped. He looked back at the gate. The man with the small mouth was staring at him through the bars.

"You see," explained Dennis weakly, "I can't stand water."

The little mouth seemed to twist into a smirk.

Dennis took a deep breath, closed his eyes, and edged round the puddle. As soon as he got to the other side he felt much better. He turned round to give the man a triumphant wave – but the man had gone.

In a Hole

··

Dennis shrugged and set off towards the
scritch-thud sound. He stepped between two
bushes and came across Colonel Hardley-
Skint himself. Or rather he came across half
of him. The Colonel was standing in a hole in
the middle of his vast lawn.

The *scritch-thud, scritch-thud* was the sound
of the Colonel digging.

The Colonel had a red face and a fierce
frown, but he was rather fond of Dennis,
and not as grumpy as he looked. His beard
was all fluffed up and, standing in his
hole, he looked something like a hairy palm
tree.

"What ho, Dennis!" he said. "Nice day."

"Greetings, Colonel. Can I help?"

Dennis liked to help. His teachers
sometimes wrote that about him. 'Dennis

always tries to be helpful.' Some of them underlined the word 'tries'.

"Help?" asked the Colonel. "How?"

"Well, you're in a hole."

Colonel Hardley-Skint looked down.

"By George, so I am. That explains it."

"Explains what?"

"Why you're looking so tall today."

He frowned his puzzled frown and stared at Dennis's knees.

"What do you think, Dennis? A nice round hole, is it?"

"Roundish, Colonel Hardley-Skint."

"Roundish. Oh dear. Oh dear, oh dear, oh dear. It ought to be perfectly round."

"What's it doing there?" Dennis asked.

"I dug it. I wanted a nice round hole so I gave the Garden Centre a tinkle and asked them to deliver one. Anyway, they said they didn't stock holes. Not enough shelf space, I suppose. They told me I'd have to dig it myself. So I did."

Dennis helped the Colonel climb out of his

hole and they stood there for a while looking at it.

"It's very good," said Dennis. "For a beginner."

"Thank you, young man," said the Colonel brightly. "I must admit the old think-box wasn't entirely on the job, though."

"Why not?"

"I've been worrying about my pictures again."

"What's wrong with them?"

"Nothing. They're jolly fine and jolly pretty. But I've spotted a strange black-haired blighter lurking about the grounds. Might've been a con man, I thought."

"I think I've just seen him, Colonel."

"Really? What was he doing?"

"Treading on me."

"Treading on you? Didn't say anything about pictures, did he?"

"No."

"That's all right, then. But you never know, young Dennis, you never know."

The Colonel scowled for a moment, then he suddenly asked, "How would you feel in a hole like that?"

"What, standing in it?"

"No, no. Of course not. Living in it. How would you feel living in a hole like that?"

Dennis thought about it, but not for long.

"Not very happy," he said.

"Why not?"

"Well, there's nothing to do in a hole, is there? I'd get bored."

"If it had water in it you could swim about."

Dennis shuddered.

"I went on a boat to Margate once," he said, "and I was sick all the way there and all the way back. Water's horrible stuff. Even in puddles."

"Well, this hole is going to have water in it," the Colonel said firmly. "I'm going to give that Garden Centre chap another tinkle and ask him to deliver some."

Dennis saw the determined expression on the Colonel's face and swallowed. This is what they do in the army, he thought. Put people in holes to toughen them up.

"Please, Colonel Hardley-Skint," he begged. "You can't do this to me."

"What?"

"Don't put me in a hole and fill it with water. Please, I beg of you."

"Oh, Dennis," chortled Colonel Hardley-Skint. "You've got it all wrong. The hole's not for you. It's for Gilbert."

"Gilbert?" sniffed Dennis. "Who's Gilbert?"

"My goldfish."

Then Dennis remembered. He'd seen Gilbert swimming round and round all day in his little bowl, and looking at the Colonel's pictures.

"You mean, this is a pond? A pond for a goldfish?"

"Of course it is."

Dennis immediately became cheerful again.

He peered at the hole and made a few helpful suggestions.

"In that case, it could be a bit bigger," he said.

"Bigger? Do you think so?"

"Yes. Gilbert can only swim in circles in a pond this size. He might get fed up with that."

Just then, Colonel Hardley-Skint's daughter Harriet came whistling along. Harriet Hardley-Skint was the same age as Dennis, but twice as tall and nearly half as helpful. She was fond of bad jokes, but Dennis liked her all the same.

"What ho, Harriet," said Colonel Hardley-Skint. "What do you think of Gilbert's pond?"

"Well," said Harriet, stroking her chin, "I shall have to pond-er about that." Then she laughed – by herself – and added, "I think it would be a lot better if it was over there."

She pointed a few metres up the lawn. Dennis wasn't sure why. The pond would

look just the same wherever it was, he thought.

"Hmm," muttered Colonel Hardley-Skint. "Perhaps we should move it."

"You can't move a hole, Pa. You have to fill it in and start again."

"But it took me all morning."

"Don't fill it in," Dennis said brightly. "Dig a new one and then join them up."

"Why?" said Harriet.

"So Gilbert can swim from one to the other. He can swim about in the first one during the day, and then whizz along to the other one at night. It can be his bedroom."

"A bedroom pond. That's a sweet idea," said Harriet. "Gilbert would love that. Take up the spade, Pa."

And the Colonel set to work again.

Well, Well, Well

By the end of the afternoon there were two small but deep holes in Colonel Hardley-Skint's lawn. And Dennis, Harriet and the Colonel stood there looking at them.

"They're still not quite round," Dennis said. "The first one still looks a bit squashed."

Colonel Hardley-Skint considered this for a moment before deciding that Dennis was right. He jumped into the first hole and started to heave out clods of earth. Harriet and Dennis watched and, from time to time, called out advice.

"A bit more off this side," said Harriet.

"And a bit more off there," Dennis added.

The Colonel's spade worked steadily and the clods began to pile up on the lawn. *Scritch-thud, scritch-thud.*

"Warm work, this," muttered the Colonel.

A jacket came flying out of the hole, followed, a while later, by a shirt. Colonel Hardley-Skint's head was smeared with mud and there were roots and things in his beard.

"How's this?" he said at last.

"Perfect," Dennis said brightly. "A perfect round."

"But it's twice as big as the other one now," said Harriet.

Colonel Hardley-Skint wiped the sweat from his brow.

"You're right, Harriet, my girl. They jolly well ought to be the same."

So he jumped out of the first hole and into the second.

"What we need now," Harriet said to Dennis, "is a couple of deckchairs. It's tiring work watching Pa dig, don't you think?"

They fetched the deckchairs and set them up. The digging went on, and they sat back and watched all afternoon. When the Colonel finished, they gave him a little clap.

"Two perfect round holes," Dennis said.

"Well done, Colonel."

"Now all you need is to dig a channel between them," said Harriet.

Colonel Hardley-Skint crawled out of the hole. Dennis could see his eyes blinking, but the rest of him was caked with mud.

"Good grief," said Harriet. "It's the Greater Bearded Mole!"

And she nearly fell out of her deckchair laughing.

"I'll take a bit of a breather, I think," said Colonel Hardley-Skint, crumpling gently in a heap.

"I shouldn't wait too long," advised Dennis. "It's getting quite dark."

In fact, it was well past teatime and they could hear the clump of Mrs Hardley-Skint's boots on the path behind them. She was coming to find out where they were. She had a tiny dog tucked under her arm like bag-pipes. The dog's name was Victoria and she wore ribbons and a little purple vest.

"Coo-ee!" trilled Mrs Hardley-Skint.

Then she caught sight of her husband stretched out on the lawn. It wasn't what she'd been expecting. Dennis could tell because she screamed.

Dennis ground his teeth together and Harriet pulled her hat down over her ears. Victoria started yapping and Colonel Hardley-Skint jumped to his feet, staggered round in a circle, and fell back into the hole again.

Mrs Hardley-Skint had a very powerful scream.

Of course, once Harriet and Dennis explained, she stopped screaming and began to chuckle.

"He's digging a pond," said Harriet. "See. Living-room there and bedroom there."

"How lovely," said Mrs Hardley-Skint. "Where's the kitchen?"

"By George," came a muffled voice from the hole. "Spot on, Ivy. You're right! We ought to give the poor little chap a kitchen."

* * *

And that was how, by the following day, there came to be three holes in the lawn. Three large, round holes.

Well, well, well. That's what Harriet said. It was a sort of Harriet-type joke. Well, well, well: three holes in the ground.

It was very impressive but Dennis wondered whether they had gone a little too far.

"After all," he said, "Gilbert is a simple goldfish. If you give him three rooms he'll only get confused."

"Nonsense," said Mrs Hardley-Skint sharply.

She was a warm and friendly lady most of the time, but Dennis sometimes found her rather bossy.

"He's only got a tiny mind," he explained. "He'll strain it if he has to decide which room to swim into."

"Nonsense," she said again. "*You've* got a tiny mind, Dennis. In fact, Gilbert hasn't got enough rooms. He should have a dining-room, a playroom and a bathroom."

"A bathroom?" said Dennis. "For a goldfish?"

"Yes. In case he needs a shower," said Harriet.

They argued about this for a while but Mrs Hardley-Skint was determined that Gilbert should have the best. And Colonel Hardley-Skint knew in his heart that there would be a lot more digging ahead.

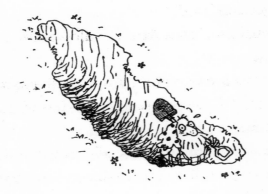

Gilbert

....

Mrs Hardley-Skint told Dennis and Harriet
to go up to Hardley-Skint Hall to see Gilbert.
"I've already seen Gilbert," said Harriet,
"and I want to stay here and watch Pa
digging."

"Of course you must see Gilbert,"
explained Mrs Hardley-Skint. "Someone has
to tell him he's about to move house."

"Why can't Victoria do it?"

"She's a doggie, Harriet. She can't talk to a
goldfish. Use your loaf, girl."

So up to Hardley-Skint Hall they went.
They found Gilbert in his usual place – in the
bowl on the large table in the library. He was
swimming slowly backwards and forwards,
curling and flicking his tail as he turned.

"How's tricks, Gilbert?" said Harriet.

Gilbert flicked and turned, flicked and
turned. His little eye swivelled.

There were two large portraits on the library wall. One showed a glum old gentleman in a feathery hat, and the other showed a lady in a dress like a hot-air balloon with a limp dog under one arm. These were Sir Jasper Hardley-Skint, and Lady Honoria Hardley-Skint. Gilbert seemed to be turning from one to the other.

"Poor old Gilbert," whispered Dennis. "He looks bored stiff."

"He does, doesn't he?" said Harriet. "He'll be much better off in the pond."

They moved in front of the pictures. Gilbert kept on turning, as if he could see through them.

"Tell him, then," said Harriet, nudging Dennis.

"Can I have a word, Gilbert?" said Dennis. "If you could just face this way a moment."

"It's no good *telling* him, Dennis. He won't understand. You'll have to show him."

"Good idea."

Dennis made his face look miserable and

mimed swimming slowly between the two pictures. Gilbert's eye swivelled in his direction. Then Dennis gave a little jump and started to swim all over the library. Breast-stroke, crawl, backstroke. All with a broad smile on his face.

"I don't think Gilbert does the backstroke," said Harriet.

"It doesn't matter, Harriet. He's getting the idea."

And certainly Gilbert had stopped gliding backwards and forwards, and seemed to be staring at Dennis. Dennis pointed at him and nodded.

"You, Gilbert," he said. "Big pond. Plenty swim."

Then he stopped miming. He held his stomach.

"What's the matter now?" said Harriet.

"Plenty swim," said Dennis in a low voice. "Water, Harriet. I don't feel very well..."

Gilbert watched blankly as Harriet led him to the bathroom.

Leaf It To Us

After five more busy days, there were six
large holes in the lawn, joined by ten deep
channels. All the earth Colonel Hardley-
Skint had dug out had been piled up into a
hefty mountain. Mrs Hardley-Skint, Victoria,
Harriet and Dennis were standing on this
mountain, looking down.

"Yes," said Mrs Hardley-Skint with a nod.
"That's more like it."

"Hmm," said Harriet. "Not bad. Not bad
at all."

"There's not much lawn left," Dennis
pointed out.

In fact, there were five small triangles of
lawn left. And you couldn't reach them.
What they needed, of course, were six little
bridges. They turned to Colonel Hardley-
Skint to make this helpful suggestion, but the

Colonel was flat on his back, staring at the sky. When Dennis shook him he just rolled over and moaned.

"I only wanted a little pond," he said.

"Nonsense," said Mrs Hardley-Skint. "If you're too lazy to put up a few bridges, I'll do it myself."

She tucked Victoria under one arm and stalked off down the mountain. Minutes later she returned with a plank. She put the plank over one of the channels and told Harriet to walk across.

"What for, Ma?" said Harriet.

"Because I want to see what happens, of course."

"Why can't Victoria do it?"

"Don't be cruel, Harriet. She might fall in."

So Harriet jumped on the plank and immediately the triangle of lawn at the other end collapsed. She skidded downwards and rolled about at the bottom.

"Just as I thought," said Mrs Hardley-Skint. "It's not strong enough. Gilbert will have to have one very big room, I think. All the lawn will have to go."

They rubbed Colonel Hardley-Skint's face with a wet flannel and told him he hadn't quite finished. He grumbled a bit but Mrs Hardley-Skint told him not to make a fuss.

"It's not fair of you to put your own comfort before Gilbert's, is it now?" she said.

The Colonel sighed, picked up his spade, and crawled towards the nearest hole.

"Go and have a bath, Harriet," said Mrs Hardley-Skint. "Dennis and I are off to the Garden Centre to get some professional advice."

"Are we?" said Dennis.

"Of course we are. Come along."

The Garden Centre was a new one. It was called:

Leaf It To Us

and there was a freshly-painted sign outside which said:

EVERYTHING FOR YOUR GARDEN, PATIO AND POND

EXPERT HELP FROM OUR TRAINED STAFF
MANAGER: PHIL BUCKETT

"In we go," said Mrs Hardley-Skint, and in they went.

They found themselves in a large greenhouse full of shrubs and flowers and trees, but there wasn't a soul in sight to help them. It was warm and damp in the greenhouse and Dennis felt there was something a little bit creepy about it. He wasn't sure what, but he began to be uneasy.

"I think there's someone around," he whispered. "I have a feeling we're being watched."

"Nonsense," said Mrs Hardley-Skint. "If there was anyone here they'd come out and serve us."

But Dennis was not convinced. He was about to say so when he caught sight of the strangest bush he'd ever seen. It was fluffy and orange – and it was on the move.

"Look out, Mrs Hardley-Skint!" he yelled. "It's a man-eating plant! Keep back, keep back!"

"Don't be silly, Dennis," said Mrs Hardley-Skint in a calm voice. "It's not a man-eating plant at all."

"It is! It is! It's coming to get us, I tell you!"

"Nonsense. It's a plant-eating man."

She moved some leaves aside and there indeed was a man with bright red hair and a black beard, chewing a carrot. Dennis calmed down at once. In fact, he felt a bit silly. Mrs Hardley-Skint told him to pull himself together and stop wailing. He was upsetting Victoria.

"Are you with Leaf It To Us?" she asked the man.

"Indeed I am," he said. "My name is

Buckett. Phil Buckett. Doctor Phil Buckett.
What do you want?"

"We've got a pond and we want some
advice."

"How big is it?"

"About from here to ... there."

Mrs Hardley-Skint narrowed her eyes and
pointed into the distance.

"My word," said Phil Buckett with a
whistle. "That's not a pond. That's a lake."

A lake, thought Dennis and swallowed. It
hadn't occurred to him before.

A lake.

Like the sea.

Like the greasy, grey, choppy water all the
way to Margate and back.

The very thought made him want to
throw up.

Beard Wobble

....

"What I suggest," suggested Phil Buckett, "is
that I come and have a look at this lake of
yours. Where is it?"

"The Hall," said Mrs Hardley-Skint.

"The hall? That's a mistake, if you don't
mind me saying so."

"Why?"

"Well, if you have a lake in a hall, people
are going to fall in and get wet when they
come through the door."

"Nonsense," said Mrs Hardley-Skint. "Not
in the hall – *at* the Hall. Hardley-Skint Hall.
The lake's outside, where the lawn used to
be."

"Ah!" said Dr Buckett and his eyes
twinkled.

"Do you know it?" Mrs Hardley-Skint
asked.

"What, Hardley-Skint Hall? Colonel Hardley-Skint's place? Where they have all those valuable old pictures? No. I can't say I've ever heard of it."

But something – he couldn't say what – told Dennis he was lying.

By the time they got back, the Colonel had finished digging and was fast asleep at the bottom of one massive hole. Phil Buckett stood gazing at it and stroking his beard thoughtfully. It seemed to wobble from side to side. And that mass of red hair appeared to lift and fall slightly on his head.

This doesn't look at all right to me, thought Dennis.

"Hmm," said Phil Buckett in an expert kind of way.

Then he clambered up the mountain and stared at the hole from the top.

"Well," said Mrs Hardley-Skint. "What do you think?"

"It's quite a good lake, I grant you," he called down.

"Of course it is," Dennis said. "We've put a lot of work into it."

"You need to put more than work into it, my little friend," said Phil Buckett.

Dennis objected to being called a "little friend". Especially by someone with bright red hair sticking out all over the place. Bright red hair that went up and down. And a beard that wobbled.

"What else do we need to put into it?" Mrs Hardley-Skint asked.

"Water."

"Well, I know that. I'm not a fool."

"But you can't use just any old water, madam," he chuckled.

"What sort of water do we need?" she asked.

"It needs what we in the garden business call 'lake water'. Whatever else you do, don't be tricked into using pond water. Pond water is for ponds, but lakes need lake water."

"That sounds reasonable," said Mrs Hardley-Skint.

"It is, madam. And it just so happens that we had a delivery of lake water only yesterday. That's reasonable too."

"How reasonable?"

"Very. Ten pence a bucket."

"How many buckets will we need?"

"Let me see," he said. "I should say roughly, give or take a bucket or two, about twenty thousand."

Twenty thousand buckets of water! Dennis turned pale at the thought. And Victoria started yapping and shaking her ribbons.

"Don't you worry, my poppet," said Mrs Hardley-Skint soothingly to the little dog. "We wouldn't let you get wet, would we? Now, let me see, twenty thousand buckets, that would cost about..."

She did some counting on her fingers, got lost and had to use Victoria's paws.

"Two thousand pounds," Dennis said helpfully.

"Well," said Dr Buckett, "not exactly. You see, for every thousand buckets you buy, you get one thrown in free."

"I see," said Mrs Hardley-Skint. "Then that sounds like a bargain."

"It sounds like a lot of money," Dennis said, "for one goldfish."

"Well, little man," said Phil Buckett with a sickly smile. "We can supply him a few little friends as well. And anyway," he added to Mrs Hardley-Skint, "who's in charge, you or Shorty here?"

The thought of twenty free buckets of 'lake water' was too tempting for Mrs Hardley-Skint. She ignored Dennis and shook hands with the man with the wobbly red hair and the deal was done.

The next day the Garden Centre van turned up with the first load of special lake water. Phil Buckett ran a hose from a large barrel in the back of the van to the lake. He turned a tap and the water began to flow in. After an hour it was still flowing in.

That's strange, thought Dennis. It should've run out by now. The barrel can't be that big.

Then Harriet and Mrs Hardley-Skint arrived and Phil Buckett turned his attention to them.

"Ah," he said smarmily, "this must be Colonel Hardley-Skint's tall and clever daughter. Harriet, isn't it?"

"It is," said Harriet, beaming because the man had recognized her.

"I've brought something to show you," said Phil Buckett. "Something that you'll just love."

He produced a catalogue and waved it under Harriet's nose.

"It's a catalogue. A boat catalogue."

"Boats?" said Mrs Hardley-Skint. "What do we want boats for?"

"Well, a lake is a fine thing, madam, but a boating lake is a very fine thing."

"Is it?" asked Harriet foolishly.

"But of course. What could be nicer than rowing around a lake on a pleasant summer evening?"

"I don't know," said Harriet doubtfully.

"You'd be rowing around on Gilbert's roof, wouldn't you? He might not like it."

"But you can charge people for a row round a lake," said Phil Buckett with his small sickly smile. "People will pay good money to row on a lake."

Soon Harriet and Mrs Hardley-Skint were so busy looking at pictures of boats that Dennis was able to creep away and take a closer look at that van.

Follow That Pipe

The first thing he noticed was the barrel in the back of the Leaf It To Us van. It had a 'lake water' label on it but it wasn't a proper printed label; it was handwritten. Then he saw that there were two pipes leading from the barrel. One ran down to the lake, and the other one was hidden under the van.

Dennis went to the front of the van and saw that the pipe came out between the wheels and disappeared into the woods.

"Follow that pipe, Dennis Dipp," he told himself.

He traced the pipe under some bushes and round some trees, through a flower-bed and across a path, and...

Ah-hah! Straight to a tap at the back of Hardley-Skint Hall!

'Lake water' indeed. This was Hardley-

Skint Hall tap water, and Colonel Hardley-Skint was paying ten pence a bucket for it. (He didn't know he was paying for it, of course. He was back at the Hall, snoozing away in his room.)

Dennis turned the tap off and hid himself in a bush to see what would happen next. For a while nothing did. Then he heard someone mumbling and cursing in the undergrowth, and along came Dr Phil Buckett himself.

Surprise, surprise!

Phil Buckett emerged backwards from the flower-bed, running the pipe through his hands. He backed into the tap and stood up sharply.

"Ow!"

He turned round and bent down to examine the tap.

Dennis stepped out of his bush and stood directly behind him.

"Problems with the water?" he said casually.

Phil Buckett jumped a metre in the air and

shot round to see who'd spoken. He shot round so quickly that his hair was still facing the other way.

Good grief! A wig! No wonder his hair moved.

With the wig on back to front, the man was having trouble seeing Dennis. He tried to set it right but only managed to dislodge the beard. It fell from his face like a small curtain and hung from one ear. Then the wig slipped off entirely and Dennis saw that the hair beneath was black and shiny.

It was the man who'd smirked through the bars of the gate. He glared at Dennis and curled his lip.

"Get lost, Shorty!" he said.

"Don't call me that. I'm not short, I'm young."

"All kids are shorties," said Phil Buckett with a sneer.

In fact, Dennis was a bit on the short side and one of his ambitions was to be much taller. But Harriet and her parents liked

Dennis the way he was, and being short didn't stop him being cheery or helpful. None of this meant anything to Phil Buckett, though.

"Shorty Short-pants," he jeered.

"And you're a nasty rotten rotter," Dennis shouted back. It was all he could think of at the time. "You're up to something, I know you are!"

"And you, Dennis Dipp, are down to something!"

Dennis was stung.

"That's a rotten joke," he said. "Even Harriet could do better than that."

"Shove off!"

"I'm telling the Colonel on you."

"He won't take any notice of a twit like you."

"Pilchard!" said Dennis.

"Buffoon!" Phil Buckett answered.

"Louse!" Dennis retorted.

"Titch!" Phil Buckett responded.

Before Dennis could take his turn, they

heard a yapping in the woods, and Phil Buckett slapped his wig back on.

"Lovely boats, Dr Buckett," said Mrs Hardley-Skint striding up to them. "I think we might be able to talk Colonel Hardley-Skint into buying a few."

"Mrs Hardley-Skint," Dennis cried, "this man is up to no good!"

"Nonsense. He's being so helpful."

"No, he isn't. He's being shifty!"

"He can't be shifty," said Harriet. "He's a doctor."

"He is shifty!" Dennis shouted. "He's got a wig and wobbly beard and ... and..."

"Dennis," snapped Mrs Hardley-Skint, "you're talking drivel and you're being rude. Stop it at once!"

"But ... but ... I've seen him here before and..."

"Dennis! Heel!"

Dennis blinked and shut his mouth.

"I do apologize, Dr Buckett," said Mrs Hardley-Skint in a thin, sweet voice. "First he thought you were a man-eating plant and now he thinks you can't be trusted."

"Please," said Phil Buckett, holding up his hands. "I think I know what the problem is. You are people of class and he's a bit common..."

"I'm not, I'm not!" Dennis cried.

"I expect he's feeling a bit left out," Phil Buckett continued. "I'll tell you what: why don't we try to involve the little fellow?"

"Good idea," said Mrs Hardley-Skint. "How?"

"Let me see, let me see. I know!" Phil Buckett clicked his fingers as if he'd just had a brand-new idea. "Little Shorty here can be the first person to row across the lake."

"Not Dennis," said Harriet. "He can't stand water."

"Can't stand water?" Phil Buckett chortled. "What a wimp!"

"I'm not, I'm not!" Dennis cried again.

"You must be if you can't row across a lake."

"I can row across a lake, I can!"

"I don't think so."

"I bet I can!"

"And I bet you can't!"

"I can!"

Then Phil Buckett stopped shouting and became instantly calm and smiley.

"Well," he said. "there's one way to find out, isn't there? We'll hold a proper bet. A wager."

The Wager

Dennis stuck out his hand for Phil Buckett to shake.

"Done," he said. "Agreed!"

And, of course, at that very moment, he realized just what he'd agreed to. To sit in a boat. On the water. To row from one end of the lake to the other.

I'll be as sick as a dog, he thought. I'll never do it.

"Are you sure about this?" Harriet asked him. "You know what you're like."

"Of course I'm sure," said Dennis.

But he wasn't. He wasn't at all sure about it.

"Right," said Phil Buckett, pulling pen and paper from his pocket. "You row from one end of the lake to the other. In a little rowing-boat, with oars, not a motor."

"Agreed," said Dennis.

"And you mustn't sink..."

"Agreed."

"Or fall out of the boat..."

"Agreed."

"Or throw up?"

Dennis hesitated.

"Come on, Shorty. No throwing up."

"All right, all right. Agreed."

"Splendid!" said Mrs Hardley-Skint. "We'll have a Grand Opening. With tents and cream teas!"

"I shouldn't bother," put in Dennis. "Honestly..."

"Nonsense! We must have a Grand Opening. We'll invite the village in. And when Dennis has rowed the lake, we'll introduce Gilbert to his new home."

While Phil Buckett was writing all this down, Colonel Hardley-Skint came ambling towards them, rubbing his eyes and yawning.

"What ho," he said. "Who's this?"

"This is Dr Buckett of the Garden Centre,"

explained Mrs Hardley-Skint. "And he's selling you some boats for the lake."

"Lake?" blinked the Colonel. "What lake?"

"The pond, dear. It's not a pond apparently, it's a lake. And we're having a Grand Opening and young Dennis here will be the first to row across, and everyone will cheer, and then we'll have a little ceremony and Gilbert can move in."

Colonel Hardley-Skint pulled a puzzled face and tried to catch up.

"But Dennis," he said, "what about Margate?"

"Oh," said Dennis with a weak chuckle. "Don't worry about that."

"Sure?"

"Absolutely."

"Right-oh, then," said the Colonel with a slap of his thigh. "What's the deal?"

"Well," said Phil Buckett, "what shall we say? If the little lad wins, you can have my complete supply of lake water free."

"Free! I say! Most generous."

"And if he loses?" asked Mrs Hardley-Skint.

"Let me see, let me see," said Phil Buckett, scratching his wig with his pen. "I know! The very thing. A few pictures for my wall! You wouldn't happen to have a few pictures, would you, Colonel Hardley-Skint?"

"I have, yes," the Colonel said doubtfully, "but they're jolly pretty ones and I don't want to lose them."

"Oh, so you think that Shorty here will lose, do you?"

"Of course not. You said you wouldn't lose, didn't you, Dennis, old man?"

"Well…" said Dennis.

"So your pictures aren't in danger, are they?" Phil Buckett put in.

"No, I suppose they're not. Very well, Dr Buckett. It's a deal."

"Splendid!" said Phil Buckett. "We'll do it on Thursday."

He gave the pen and paper to the Colonel.

"Sign here."

And the Colonel signed. Phil Buckett went off, whistling happily to himself, and the others turned to look at Dennis. He smiled feebly at them.

"Well, young Dennis," said Mrs Hardley-Skint, punching him cheerfully on the shoulder, "it's up to you now."

"Yes," he said. "I am a tiny bit worried, though."

"Why?"

"It's the not-throwing-up bit. I'm not absolutely sure I can manage that."

"Then why did you say you could?"

"I got carried away."

Mrs Hardley-Skint set her lips and frowned at him.

"You will be carried away, Dennis, if you let us down now. I'll carry you away myself."

"I have to be honest, though, Mrs H. Water does make me feel sick."

"And you make me feel sick."

"But..."

"No. Don't argue," insisted Mrs Hardley-Skint. "You can't be sick. You'll just have to overcome it. Be a man, Dennis."

"I don't want to be a man. Not yet. I'm quite happy being a boy."

"Don't worry, laddie," said the Colonel. "You'll love it really. Bobbing about on the fresh open water…"

Dennis tried to protest. He opened his mouth to speak, but the very thought of bobbing about on any kind of water put his head in a spin and churned his stomach. He threw up.

"Oh, good gracious!" said Mrs Hardley-Skint. "You poor, poor thing!"

"I'll be all right in a minute, Mrs Hardley-Skint," groaned Dennis.

"Not you, Dennis. Poor little Victoria. You've splashed her, look. How could you be so thoughtless?"

Dennis groaned again.

"I say," said Colonel Hardley-Skint. "This looks bad."

"Bad?" screeched his wife. "It's utterly disgusting!"

"No, no, my little honeysuckle. I don't mean the doggie. I mean Dennis. The doggie doesn't mind a bit of sick, do you, doggie?"

A low-pitched growl came from the back of Victoria's throat. Her tiny flat face scowled as her mistress dabbed away with a lace hanky.

"How would you like it, then?" snapped Mrs Hardley-Skint. "Dennis, be sick on Colonel Hardley-Skint and see how he likes it."

"No, Dennis," warned Harriet. "Better not. I bought Pa that tie."

"The thing is," said the Colonel, "if the *thought* of water makes young Dennis sick, how is he going to row across the lake?"

They all fell silent and pondered this. The Colonel tugged his ear and shook his head.

"There's no doubt about it," he said, "we're in another hole now."

Plans, Plans

....

"We'll have to call it off," said Mrs Hardley-Skint.

"Impossible, sugarplum," the Colonel told her. "I've signed my name and I can't go back on my word."

"This is your fault, Dennis," Harriet put in. "If you'd only kept your mouth shut..." Dennis's voice came out in a squeak.

"Me?"

"Yes. And you ought to do something about it. Like row across the lake and stop making such a fuss."

"I'll be sick, though."

The Colonel's wife snorted.

"Nonsense. You don't have to be sick if you don't want to be."

"But I can't help it, Mrs H. And if I'm sick, we'll lose the wager..."

"And if we lose the wager," Harriet said, "we lose the pictures."

They stopped arguing and thought for a while. They thought about Sir Jasper and Lady Honoria and all the other old Hardley-Skints. Removed from their rightful home.

"Oh, tish," said the Colonel. "Tish, tish, tish!"

"Tish?" snapped his wife. "That's a helpful suggestion, I must say. What we need is a proper plan, not someone spouting 'Tish' all the time."

So they returned to the Hall where they sat down, each in a different room and in total silence, and tried to think. Dennis went to the library and watched Gilbert gliding backwards and forwards, backwards and forwards, in his tiny bowl.

"What do you think, Gilbert?" he asked. "What am I going to do?"

Gilbert moved his lips and gawped back at Dennis. But he had nothing to suggest.

He just looked blank and Dennis felt sorry for him.

By teatime Dennis hadn't come up with a single idea. He wandered miserably down to the lounge and found the others waiting for him in silence.

"At last," said Harriet. "Now we can begin."

"You first, Hat," said her mother.

"Well," went on Harriet, "it's quite easy when you think about it. All we have to do is tape up his mouth."

"But that's horrible," said Dennis.

"You wouldn't be sick, though."

"Yes, he would, dear," said Mrs Hardley-Skint. "It would just stay inside, that's all."

"It might come out of his ears or something," suggested the Colonel with a frown. "And then what happens to the pictures?"

They thought about this for a short while and then decided to move on to Mrs Hardley-Skint's idea.

"If we starve him today and tomorrow," she

said, "he won't have anything to be sick with."

The Colonel shook his head.

"He will, sweetikins. I've seen men be sick on an empty stomach."

"But not real sick, surely, dear?"

"It was pretty sicky-looking stuff, my poppet, I can promise you. I'm sure Dr Buckett will think it's real sick."

"And anyway," said Dennis, "I need my food."

"That's true," said Harriet. "He must eat to get his strength up. Perhaps we'd better hear your idea, Pa."

"Right-oh. By far the best way is to get young Dennis here used to water."

"How?" they chorused.

"Build him up gradually. Show him pictures of it. Take him for walks across puddles. Sit him in a bath and make waves. Make him go for a paddle..."

Dennis made a gagging sound.

"Stop, dear!" Mrs Hardley-Skint ordered her husband. "Stop at once or he'll be off like a fountain."

She tucked Victoria under her arm for safety.

"But it might just work," insisted Colonel Hardley-Skint.

"No," moaned Dennis, "it won't. I know it won't."

"Come, come, old man. You might be violently sick for a couple of days, but you'll get used to it in the end. That's the point."

"A couple of days!" cried Mrs Hardley-Skint. "We don't want to be skidding around in sick for a couple of days. Have some consideration for little Victoria here."

So that was three ideas shot down in flames. They turned to Dennis and there were questions in their faces. Dennis smiled sadly.

"Sorry," he said, "I couldn't think of a thing."

"You great soft pudding," said Mrs Hardley-Skint.

The Colonel sighed, long and low, and they all sat in a silent circle, looking at the floor.

Mrs Hardley-Skint took up her knitting again and the others doodled on their bits of paper. The light began to fade and the lounge became quite dark.

"This is no good," said the Colonel, throwing his pencil down in disgust. "We've thought and thought and we've come up with nothing."

Mrs Hardley-Skint gave Victoria a squeeze and said, "I say, dear, we haven't asked Victoria here yet."

"She's welcome to chip in if she likes, sweetie-pie."

Victoria was sitting on a cushion staring at a plate of cakes. Staring blankly, like Gilbert in his bowl. Her brown eyes were big and round, as if she were in a trance.

In a trance, thought Dennis. In a trance...

And he sat there in a trance of his own for several seconds. Then he blinked.

"That's it," he said. "Victoria has come up with an idea, and I think it might just work."

Trance

"What do you notice about Victoria?" Dennis asked. "What does she look like?"

"Dim," said Harriet.

"Blank," said the Colonel.

"Sweet," said Mrs Hardley-Skint.

"No, no," Dennis put in. "She looks as if she's in a trance. She looks as if she's been hypnotized."

"So what?" said Harriet. "She looks like that most of the time."

"But hypnotized! Don't you see?"

And then Dennis explained Victoria's idea, or rather, the idea that Victoria had given him. It was this. Why shouldn't he, Dennis Dipp, be hypnotized?

"Fiddle-faddle," said Colonel Hardley-Skint. "Doggies can't hypnotize people."

"No, Pa," Harriet said. "He's right. People

are hypnotized to get over their fear of snakes and things. Perhaps it'll work with water, too. It's brilliant, Dennis!"

"It is a brilliant idea," admitted Mrs Hardley-Skint, "but of course, it's really Victoria's."

She patted the little dog and fed her a piece of cake – a thing she was never usually allowed. So Victoria knew she'd done something rather wonderful, though she wasn't quite sure what.

They looked in the phone book under "H" for hypnotists and found just one: "A. Maze – spoon juggler and hypnotist: put your mind in my hands".

The Colonel still thought it was fiddle-faddle, but he made the call and A. Maze's secretary said nothing could be done until the day after tomorrow.

In the meantime, they set about making arrangements for Thursday's Grand Opening. The Colonel said there was no need for arrangements. He didn't want

crowds of people to see young Dennis
being sick and falling out of boats. But Mrs
Hardley-Skint reminded him about his
promise to invite allcomers.

"And a promise is a promise," she said, "so
we'll have to let people know."

So next morning the Colonel walked
gloomily into the village to put a postcard in
the window of the little paper shop.

It said, in small, faint writing:

Dennis Dipp will row across Gilbert's pond
on Thursday. If he makes it, Gilbert (my goldfish)
will be introduced to his new home. You
can come if you like, but I know there's
a nice quiz show on the TV so if you want
to stay in and watch that, I won't mind a bit.

Yours, Colonel H-S.

"How long do you want it in the window?"
said the man in the shop. "One week or two?"

"Half an hour," muttered the Colonel, and
hurried back to the Hall.

On the Wednesday, A. Maze turned up on the dot of nine o'clock. The first thing they noticed about her was that she was a woman. The "A" stood for Ada. She was young, with a green and orange flowing dress, a sweet round face and glasses. The Colonel looked at her with deep suspicion.

"Be warned, young Dennis," he muttered as Ada was shown into the library. "Never put your mind in the hands of a pretty woman. I've never had anything to do with pretty women in all my life."

"And I have never had anything to do with handsome men," said his wife tartly.

A brief row followed and, by the time they joined Ada in the library, she was sitting in the Colonel's armchair fast asleep.

"There," said the Colonel, "what did I tell you? She's dozed off – in my chair. Useless."

"No, Colonel," said Ada without opening her eyes. "I am wide awake. I am merely trying to pick up the vibes of the place."

"We are a tidy family," Mrs Hardley-Skint

sniffed. "We do not leave vibes lying around in the library..."

"She means vibrations, Mrs Hardley-Skint," explained Dennis.

"Precisely," said Ada. "And the vibes in here are very jittery. I see someone with a name beginning with 'G'. And he is very worried at the moment."

"G," said Harriet. "That's Gilbert!"

"But it's young Dennis here who needs your help," explained Mrs Hardley-Skint.

Ada opened one eye and looked at Dennis.

"Yes," she said. "I can see that now. Would you like to use your own spoons, or the ones I've brought with me?"

"We don't want him to juggle spoons, Miss Maze," said the Colonel with a tut. "That's not going to help, is it?" And he added in a loud whisper, "What did I tell you? Useless."

Ada removed her glasses with a flourish.

"Look into my eyes, then," she said.

Dennis could only see one eye so he looked into that. It was green and seemed to sparkle.

"Your arms are becoming heavy," Ada said in a soft voice. "So – so – heavy."

The other eye flicked open. This one was blue and it fixed Dennis like a skewer, like a beam from a torch. His arms became heavy. The library blurred and faded and all he could see were two deep pools, one blue and one green. They swam into each other.

"You are no longer Dennis Dipp," the voice intoned.

Dennis stopped being Dennis and waited to find out what he was instead.

"You are a cat. A frisky little cat."

Dennis mewed. He licked his paw and rubbed his face with it. He caught sight of the ball of wool at Mrs Hardley-Skint's feet and made a dive at it. It rolled under the sofa and Dennis charged after it. This was fun. His ears pricked. He rolled over on his back and tried to hook the wool up in his claws.

Then Ada lifted her hand dramatically. There was a loud click as she snapped her fingers and Dennis came out of his trance.

He was shocked and embarrassed to find himself on the floor playing with a ball of wool. He sat up and looked around. Harriet and Mrs Hardley-Skint were staring at him with open mouths.

"My good gracious," said Harriet quietly. "It works."

"Maybe so," said the Colonel, "but what's the use of it? Cats don't like water."

"Why should they?" asked Ada.

So they explained about the wager.

"You should have told me before," she said. "I can remove the fear of water with no trouble at all."

She sat Dennis in the armchair and put him into another trance.

Unmasked

....

On Thursday, at breakfast, Dennis chattered
on and on about water until the Hardley-
Skints were heartily sick of it.

"Lovely! Lovely!" he cried, filling his glass
from a jug on the table. "Lovely, splashy wet-
wet water! Whee! Oooh! SPLASH! Lovely!
Lovely!"

"There's no need to overdo it," said Mrs
Hardley-Skint, but Dennis took no notice.

He took a mouthful and dribbled it down
his chin.

"Oooh-aaahh! Blubber-lubber-lub!" he
cried. "It's LUBBERLY!"

They removed the jug and he began to tuck
into a huge plate of fried bread and eggs.

"Are you sure that's wise, young Dennis?"
Colonel Hardley-Skint asked him.

"I have to get my strength up, Colonel,"

said Dennis, chomping away like the back of a dustcart.

The Colonel sighed and glanced at his wife. She was busy making notes on the back of an envelope.

"How many chairs shall I set out?" she asked.

"Four," he told her.

"Nonsense, dear. We'll need a lot more than that."

"No we won't, honeybun," he said, remembering his postcard message. "One each for us, and one for the crowd."

"What about old Buckett?" asked Harriet.

"I won't be asking him to sit down, Harriet."

But when they went down to the lake, they found hundreds of people milling about in their best clothes. There were picnic baskets and folding chairs all over the place. Word had got round and everybody wanted to see Dennis Dipp row the lake.

Phil Buckett was already there, topping up

Gilbert's pond with a final barrel of lake water. He also had a megaphone, a small, rickety boat for Dennis to row in, and a heavy wooden crate.

"What's that for?" asked Mrs Hardley-Skint.

"To take the pictures away in," grinned Phil Buckett.

"Oh, ho," said Harriet, "I shouldn't be so cocky if I were you. Dennis will do his stuff all right."

"We'll see, we'll see," said Phil Buckett, and he hummed away to himself as he got things ready.

"I say!" said Colonel Hardley-Skint. "You've shaved, and you've had your hair done. It's changed colour and gone all straight."

"No it hasn't. I've just taken my wig off."

"A wig? Why should you wear a wig?"

"In case you recognized me," smiled Phil Buckett.

The Hardley-Skints frowned and looked

more closely at him. By George, they did recognize him now. The Colonel had seen that face with its shiny black hair lurking about in the grounds, and Mrs Hardley-Skint had seen it in the papers.

"You're not Phil Buckett at all!" she cried. "You're Stanley Gossage, aren't you?"

"WHAT?" bellowed the Colonel.

"Stanley Gossage?" said Harriet. "Who's Stanley Gossage?"

"Stanley Gossage the art dealer," snorted Mrs Hardley-Skint. "And don't deny it. I know that's who you are!"

"You're dead right, my dear."

"It's no good wriggling your way out of it..."

"I'm not."

"You are Stanley Gossage! Admit it!"

"I do."

"You do?"

"Yes. No need to pretend now. I am."

"But you're a con man! They said so in the papers."

"You can't believe everything you read in

the papers. And, anyway, the Colonel has signed and he can't go back on it now. I shall win the wager and take your pictures away and there's nothing you can do about it."

"You blighter," said Colonel Hardley-Skint.

"Indeed," agreed Stanley Gossage. "But you must admit, I'm a clever blighter."

Mrs Hardley-Skint glowered and turned to Dennis.

"This is your fault," she said. "You knew he was wearing a wig. Why didn't you say something?"

"I did," protested Dennis, "but you wouldn't listen."

"It doesn't matter now," said Harriet, "because he's going to win the bet. Aren't you, Dennis?"

"Of course I am."

"Are you indeed?" asked Stanley Gossage.

He smirked horribly and pulled on a pair of bright yellow rubber gloves.

"Don't want to get our hands wet, do we, Shorty?" he said with a wink.

"I do," said Dennis.

"What, Diddy Dennis Dipp, getting his hands wet? Dipp the Drip, who's so afraid of water?"

"How do you know that?" said the Colonel.

"Because he told me himself. And that's exactly why I suggested this wager."

"I *was* afraid," said Dennis smugly. "But I'm not now. Lovely, splashy wet-wet dribbles! Oh yes. Shall we begin?"

He trotted up and down on the spot and did a few limbering up exercises. The crowd began to gather round. Stanley Gossage glared suspiciously at Dennis.

"I don't believe you, Shorty!" he said. "Put one foot in that boat and you'll throw up."

"No, he won't," said Harriet, "because he's been put in a trance."

"Rubbish!"

"It's true," Dennis said with a smile. "I love water now, and I can't wait to get in that boat."

"But that's cheating!"

"Nonsense," barked Mrs Hardley-Skint. "Trances are perfectly fair."

Dennis sprang cheerfully into the little boat and pushed away from the shore. The crowd waved their hats and scarves and cheered.

"Yo-heave-HO!" Dennis cried merrily, and grabbed hold of the oars.

Snap

Stanley Gossage, purple with rage, threw down the megaphone, shook his fists and jumped up and down.

"Not fair, not fair, NOT FAIR! Trances are NOT FAIR!"

"Row, row, row the boat, gently down the stream," Dennis sang as he struck out across Gilbert's pond. "Diddly-diddly, diddly-diddly, life is but a dream."

The Colonel gave him a wave and began to look more relaxed. Perhaps young Dennis would save the day after all. Then Stanley Gossage stopped jumping up and down and stood quite still, as if an idea had just struck him. Which it had.

"If he can be put into a trance," he said, "he can be taken out of it again. I've seen it done."

"Get rowing, Dennis!" yelled Harriet. "Quick!"

"All you do is click your fingers," said Stanley Gossage. "Like this."

He raised a hand and the Hardley-Skints flinched, waiting for the fateful click. It didn't come. Instead they heard a faint rubbery squeak.

"He's still got his gloves on," said Mrs Hardley-Skint.

"Oh, blither it!" said Stanley Gossage.

Dennis pulled further and futher from the shore.

Stanley Gossage yanked desperately at the gloves. They stretched but they wouldn't come off.

"Off, off, off, you beggars!" he cried.

He wedged the fingers under his foot and leaned back. The gloves were pulled so thin they turned white. Then there was a twang and a sausagey yellow blur as they whipped back and slapped him under his chin.

"YEOOW!"

But he was free of them, and he dashed down to the edge of the lake, snapping his fingers. Dennis, though, was too far away to hear, and he rowed steadfastly on.

"Snap!" yelled Stanley Gossage. "SNAP! SNAP! SNAP!"

But saying "snap" is not the same as doing it, and Dennis was more than halfway across by this time – only about twenty metres to go.

"Too late," said Harriet. "You can't stop him now."

Stanley Gossage scowled at her. Then he caught sight of the megaphone on the ground. He snatched it up and snapped his fingers into it. The snap rang out like a pistol shot.

Dennis stopped rowing.

He looked about him and saw water. Green and queasy water.

He clapped a hand to his mouth.

He began to think about fried bread and eggs. Even from the shore of the lake, everyone could tell he was thinking about fried bread and eggs.

"Ah ha!" cried Stanley Gossage. "He's done for. Go on, Shorty. Throw up!"

He took up the megaphone again and his shout became a chant.

"Go on, Shorty! Throw UP! Throw UP! Throw UP!"

He would have gone on like this, but Victoria decided it was time to play her part: she nipped him in the ankle and he dropped the megaphone. And this made all the difference. Dennis, with a hand still clasped to his mouth, grabbed one of the oars and dipped it into the lake.

"He's carrying on," cried a girl in the crowd.

"What a Trojan!" said the Colonel. "Well done, that man!"

"Well done, that doggie!" said Mrs Hardley-Skint.

But rowing with one oar doesn't really work, and the little boat began to turn in a slow circle, still twenty metres from shore.

Dennis was concentrating so hard that he didn't realize he was making no progress. Mrs Hardley-Skint snatched the megaphone and bellowed into it.

"Stop rowing, Dennis! You'll have to paddle, not row!"

The crowd fell silent as Dennis got to his feet, wobbled, teetered, nearly plunged over the side ... and ... ah! ... steadied himself. He waggled the oar over the back of the boat and it began to edge towards the far shore again.

"Good grief," muttered the Colonel, "he's as green as boiled cabbage."

With a thrash and a splash, and his cheeks puffed out like balloons, Dennis guided the boat towards the shore. Nearer ... nearer...

"Den-nis! Den-nis!" cried the crowd with one voice.

And nearer...

"Throw UP! Throw UP!" yelled Stanley Gossage.

And Dennis certainly looked as if he were on the very verge of doing just that ... when the boat bumped and stopped.

As he stumbled off it and collapsed on dry ground, he heard a rousing cheer far, far behind him.

He was sick then, of course. Rather disastrously sick. But he didn't really mind. He'd done it. All by himself.

He lifted his head and saw hundreds of people, led by the Colonel, running round the lake to congratulate him.

Absolutely Free

....

"Ladies and gentlemen," said the Colonel to the crowd, "it really is lovely to see so many of you here today!"

He was speaking through the megaphone and standing on the packing case Phil Buckett planned to use for the pictures.

"I'm sorry we didn't have quite enough chairs," went on the Colonel, "but, as I say, it really, really is..."

"Do get on with it, dear," Mrs Hardley-Skint hissed at him.

"What? Oh. Yes. Well, first of all, a big thank you to Dr Stanley Buckett-Gossage, or whatever his name is, for kindly giving us all this lovely lake water – absolutely free of charge."

There was polite clapping from the crowd. Stanley Gossage was furious but he tried to

smile. All the muscles on his face stood out, and he looked like a weight-lifter about to drop his weights. The small children in the front of the crowd hid behind the legs of their mums and dads.

"Now, Dr Phil Gossage-Buckett has also agreed to give us – absolutely free of charge – rocks and water plants and some friendly goldfish to keep Gilbert company. Haven't you, Dr Gossage-Phil-Stanley?"

"Don't keep saying that," whispered Gossage through gritted teeth.

"Saying what?"

"Absolutely free of charge."

"As I say," said the Colonel turning to the crowd, "he is giving all this – absolutely free of charge!"

More polite clapping.

"Finally, ladies and gentlemen, we come to the Grand Ceremony of Putting Gilbert in the Pond. And there's only one person who deserves the honour of doing that. May I present to you the Hero of the Hour, the

Champion of Gilbert's Pond, your own, your very own – Dennis Dipp!"

The crowd cheered and clapped their hands above their heads. Dennis turned a deep red and gave a modest bow. Then he picked up Gilbert's bowl and walked solemnly to the edge of the pond. There was a respectful hush as he lowered the bowl into the water.

Then Gilbert flicked his tail and swam off. He turned a big circle in the water, and seemed to look back at Dennis with a tiny goldfishy smile.

GLADIATORS NEVER BLINK
Nick Warburton

Eyes front for some rollicking Roman fun!

Corrina may be the most worthless slave in the villa of Aponius Saturninus, but she is also the best informed. Her latest discovery is that Bato, the smarmy slave master, is planning to make gladiators of two hapless young Britons, Diodorus and Flamma. Can Corrina help save them from a sticky end?

The laughs come thick and fast in this hilarious Roman comedy!

MY AUNTY SAL AND
THE MEGA-SIZED MOOSE
Martin Waddell

Meet Aunty Sal – the world's greatest adventurer!

There's only one thing Aunty Sal loves more than adventures – and that's telling people about them. Hear about the time she tangled with a mega-sized moose, her adventure with pirates on the Spanish Main, her showdown with Killer McGill in the Last Chance Saloon – and lots more besides.

Believe them or not, these tall tales are the funniest, most dang entertaining you could wish for!

MORE WALKER PAPERBACKS
For You to Enjoy

☐ 0-7445-6902-8   *Gladiators Never Blink*
by Nick Warburton   £3.99

☐ 0-7445-5203-6   *My Aunty Sal and
the Mega-sized Moose*
by Martin Waddell   £3.99

☐ 0-7445-4760-1   *Haunted House Blues*
by Theresa Tomlinson   £3.99

☐ 0-7445-7258-4   *Florizella and the Giants*
by Philippa Gregory   £3.99

☐ 0-7445-7718-7   *Capture by Aliens!*
by Eric Johns   £3.99

☐ 0-7445-6977-X   *Starquest: Voyage to the
Greylon Galaxy*
by Alan Durant   £3.99

☐ 0-7445-5288-5   *Broops! Down the Chimney*
by Nicholas Fisk   £3.99

☐ 0-7445-7242-8   *Bernard's Gang*
by Dick Cate   £3.99

**Walker Paperbacks are available from most booksellers,
or by post from B.B.C.S., P.O. Box 941, Hull, North Humberside HU1 3YQ**

24 hour telephone credit card line 01482 224626

To order, send: Title, author, ISBN number and price for each book ordered, your full
name and address, cheque or postal order payable to BBCS for the total amount and allow
the following for postage and packing: UK and BFPO: £1.00 for the first book, and 50p
for each additional book to a maximum of £3.50. Overseas and Eire: £2.00 for the first
book, £1.00 for the second and 50p for each additional book.

Prices and availability are subject to change without notice.

Name _____

Address _____

_____